Book of Shadows 2020

Extra Pages

By 

Jean Megaw

Dedicated to our Planet

Climate Change is occurring

Everyone on Earth needs to change their ways

Contents

Pages 5 to 28 are the same stories as in the main book "Book of Shadows 2020" This book is extra diary pages to that book. The stories are repeated in case you have only purchased this book.

The Magic of Yin Yang for Non Witches and Witches

Yin Yang is defined as two opposite yet complementary energies. Understanding this will assist you immensely in your life and your choice of pathways. For example, within this book I have given you a spell to help you understand and ease negativity. The opposite of negativity is positivity. You have both in your body to help centre you and protect you. You have both surrounding you and the universe. However sometimes negativity can take a bigger portion of control over you, and that then becomes detrimental to your wellbeing.

For your good mental health and spells to succeed a witch needs to be centred and one with themselves and the universe.

This is the Yin Yang of your body and life.

Likewise every person witch or not, needs to be centred and at one with themselves and others, otherwise they will remain in a state of chaos with everything happening all around them.

Everyday dramas will become overwhelming and made to be more powerful than what they actual are or should be. Align your Ying Yang and you will become at one with yourself and others around you. Being at one with yourself is important for your health and mental health.

.

What is a Skip Diary©™

It's your book of shadows diary, it's about having no blank pages in your diary, thoughts or spell entries. It is about not wasting the pages of your diary. Being more conscious with our environment. It's similar to being kind with our environment for example, turning lights off when not needed to conserve energy.

A blank page in your diary is similar to a blank page in your life. And your diary needs to be charged with positivity, regardless of wither you record a negative or positive feeling. You should record what you want! Even negative feelings have a place in your diary, because you can take these negative feelings and re-visit them.

And from this you shall have the ability to transform negative into positivity by using your magic for your future. By keeping your writings page by page you remove the darkness from your diary, you remove any negativity that can creep into the fabric of the blank pages. Your book will become charged with positivity regardless of how often you write in it.

How can unwritten negativity enter my book? Negativity can enter your book on its own after you write your first word. However, negativity cannot enter the blank pages that have still to be written on (It can only enter the pages in between what you have written, example in a traditional diary you write on the pages in date order, therefore if you don't write on any particular date you have a blank page in-between. With the Skip diary you will never have any blank pages in-between, unless you choose otherwise.)

Sometimes you don't feel like writing a diary entry. That's Ok, so the next entry will be next to the last one you wrote and so on. By doing that there will be no more blank pages in between your entries. Why is that important? By doing so your writings will become more energetic, positive and fulfilling. No longer do you have to waste pages, all your entries will be next to each other.

You begin writing from the first diary page, then the next time you write an entry it will be on the next page and so forth. You can use your diary entries to write spells, ideas or anything that pops into your mind. Just don't forget to put a date on the page, that's only so you look back at your past with a date in mind. If you do forget or don't want to date the page don't worry, time is immaterial in our existence.

You can use one page per day or one page for two or more days. This book has 133 skip shadow diary pages. Do with them as ye will.

Your Skip Diary will develop into your past, present and future, enjoy your writing and most of all have fun and enjoy what you do.

If you write negative feelings in your diary, then use your magic to transform them into positivity for your future. By acknowledging your negative thoughts, you have accepted that you can become positive again. Do not give your negative thoughts any meaning, nor push them away. To push them away or give them meaning will allow those thoughts to consume you and they will continue to come back and haunt you. Simply acknowledge such negative thoughts as you write them down. Then cast the magic spell that you will create.

Spell to Remove Negativity

Tools required: sage incense stick and your spell or chant.

How to carry out your spell:

Ok, two methods: First, in all instances you will light the incense stick let the smoke rise for one minute while you give your negative thoughts acknowledgement *(This is an important stage, you are purely acknowledging that they exist, but give them no importance.)* Extinguish the sage stick

Now choose method 1 or 2 depending on what applies.

Method 1 applies if you have written a negative thought or feeling into your diary. Open your diary at the page you have written your negativity. Then take the sage stick and rub the ashes into the 'Pentagon' located at the bottom of your skip diary page. Then say your spell chant as below.

Method 2 applies if you are feeling negative but haven't written anything down, perhaps it's just negative thoughts or you feel that the room you are in is negative. Ok, so take the stick and let the scent linger around the negative room. Now say your chant.

Turn the Negativity into Positivity Spell/Chant for Method 1 and 2:

Negativity in my mind,

Negativity is all around,

Negativity I see you, I hear you and I feel you

Negativity I love you

Negativity while you are part of me

You are blinding us can't you see?

There is a better way for us to live together

Positivity is your opposite, you can't have one without the other

I will believe in myself and negativity will wander

I will believe in myself and negativity will rejoice

I will believe in myself and negativity will turn to positivity

While Negativity has its purpose, to align me and care for me, sometimes it chooses the wrong path and fills me with pain.

But I believe in myself and I will align my negativity and it will change to positivity

Because my mistakes will not define me.

Because other people will not bring me down

Because I fully believe in myself

I fully believe in myself

I believe in myself.

Repeat these actions any time you feel negativity is taking hold of you. Remember you must believe in what you do 100%.

As long as you believe in yourself you do not need any other person to believe in you. All that matters and counts is that you are a believer in yourself.

Other people can be negative in their thoughts and comments. Take this with a pinch of salt, cast that pinch of salt over your back and believe in your own life. Rejoice that you have been given life on earth. Sometimes this life can be difficult to bear. And if your emotions or pain becomes too hard to bear write your feelings down, and talk with someone, talk with someone and talk with someone. Talk with family or a friend or a person that you can speak freely with like the Samaritans.

You are special, more special than you will ever understand. So believe in yourself.

Now here is a question for you. Who is the most special and important person in the world?

Think about it for a few minutes.

.

..

• • •

• • • •

• • • • •

• • • • • •

• • • • • • •

• • • • • • • •

• • • • • • • • •

• • • • • • • • • •

Ok are you ready for the answer?

You need the following tools:

    1- A Box

    2- A Mirror

Now you can try this on yourself, on friends or family.

Put the mirror inside the box. And ask this question to any person: Who is the most special and important person in the world?

Ask them to think about their answer but not to tell you.

Now you will say to them "I know the answer, you will see the answer to my question when you look into this box"

Everyone that looks into the box will see their own reflection.

For indeed you are a special and important person, sometimes you need yourself or someone else to remind you of that fact. Try it on someone you admire, love or someone that needs a little help in their life and see their reaction.

Now that is a magical spell that you can create, you can help it along by saying your magic tool chant. Try and make up your own magic potion and spell and cast it onto the box and the mirror before you ask someone to look into it. If someone is experiencing negativity or low self-esteem you could use the box and your negativity spell.

You will be amazed by the response you will get.

Remember - Belief

If you believe in something then it will be.

The hardest thing in life is believing in kindness, goodness, equality and freedom while the rest of the world around us are fighting.

Fighting about wealth, poverty, world trade and fighting against oppressors. Many are murdering to prove that their faith is superior to anyone else's. While this is extremely sad, it will change one day. With each new 'light' born to earth so does true knowledge come; That EVERYONE on earth are from the same, we all have the same blood, we are all family. We are all part of the universe.

Wisdom is passed down to the new 'light' on earth. If your kindness and goodness effects one person then you have indeed made a start at ending this world of madness.

I went to Africa to work, I saw poverty that I had never witnessed before, and I became distraught that I was powerless to help. My magic would not work. So I did nothing, as I did not know what I could do to help every person. Then the penny dropped, if I help one person and then another, perhaps they could do the same to others.

What I find sad, is our leaders turn away from such poverty and malnutrition. Borders are what separate 'us' from 'them', yet 'them' are 'us.'

Our society has become monetarily based to a degree of disgust.

These unfortunates are out of sight, therefore they are out of mind. Our leaders work hard at keeping their borders free from immigrants in a bid to protect their own wealth, jobs etc.

Goodness and kindness will join you on your journey of death but wealth cannot be taken with you.

Use your magic for kindness and goodness and you will have fulfilled your earthly purpose.

Happy diary writing.

Witch Jokes

Q: How is a witch like a candle?
A: They're both wick-ed.

Q: What's the difference between a broomstick
and a pumpkin?
A: You can't make a broomstick pie.

Q: Why do witches wear name tags?
A: So we can tell which witch is which!

Q: What happened to the naughty witch at school?
A: She was ex-spelled.

Q: What did the tired witch do?
A: She sat down for a spell.

Q: What do you call a witch who lives at the beach?
A: A sand-witch.

Q: What story do little witches like to hear at bedtime?
A: Ghoul-di-locks and the Three Scares.

Q: How do witches on broomsticks drink their hot tea?
A: Very carefully!

Q: What was the name of the witch with one leg?
A: Eileen.

Q: Why do witches fly on brooms?
A: Vacuum cleaner cords are too short.

Q: What do you call a witch's garage?
A: A broom closet.

Q: What do witches put on their hair?
A: Scare spray.

Q: What did the doctor say to the witch in hospital?
A: Soon you'll feel well enough to sit up for a spell.

North
West
East
South
Towards South
You

You're Skip Diary

Write in any style you want, write in any place on the page. Write within the lines or outside the lines. Write in any manner or form you want.

Write the date on the top right hand of the page, or don't. If you need more than one page then write the same date on that page as well. That way there will be no blank pages as in a normal diary. No blank pages stops negativity from forming. You can write every day, or once a week or once a month, it's totally up to you.

You can write your thoughts (negative and/or positive). But remember to try and give yourself positive solutions to any negative thoughts that day. Or come back another day and respond to your written thoughts.

This is your journal, as you put pen to paper, that will be your present, and what you write becomes your past. Your future is how you interpret your writings and how you plan to help yourself, others and your planet earth and the universe in the future. Remember your future is not yet here but it can be predicted. For example the current climate change can be predicted to get worse. However, if we act now then we can change the predicted future for a better outcome.

Use the present and past to shape your future.

By writing your thoughts, feelings and what occurred today will free you from the anxiety each day to day pressures puts on your shoulders.

About my day

Spells, Whats on my mind or anything else

DATE __/__/__

About my day

Spells, Whats on my mind or anything else

DATE __/__/__

About my day

Spells, Whats on my mind or anything else

HEY WITCH- MY SKIP DIARY

DATE __/__/__

About my day

Spells, Whats on my mind or anything else

About my day

Spells, Whats on my mind or anything else

DATE __/__/__

About my day

Spells, Whats on my mind or anything else

DATE __/__/__

About my day

____

Spells, Whats on my mind or anything else

____

DATE __/__/__

About my day

Spells, Whats on my mind or anything else

DATE __/__/__

About my day

Spells, Whats on my mind or anything else

DATE __/__/__

About my day

Spells, Whats on my mind or anything else

About my day

Spells, Whats on my mind or anything else

About my day

Spells, Whats on my mind or anything else

DATE __/__/__

About my day

Spells, Whats on my mind or anything else

DATE __/__/__

About my day

Spells, Whats on my mind or anything else

DATE __/__/__

About my day

Spells, Whats on my mind or anything else

DATE __/__/__

About my day

Spells, Whats on my mind or anything else

DATE __/__/__

About my day

Spells, Whats on my mind or anything else

DATE _ _ / _ _ / _ _

About my day

Spells, Whats on my mind or anything else

DATE __/__/__

About my day

Spells, Whats on my mind or anything else

DATE __ / __ / __

About my day

Spells, Whats on my mind or anything else

About my day

Spells, Whats on my mind or anything else

DATE __/__/__

About my day

Spells, Whats on my mind or anything else

DATE __/__/__

About my day

Spells, Whats on my mind or anything else

DATE __ / __ / __

About my day

Spells, Whats on my mind or anything else

DATE __/__/__

About my day

Spells, Whats on my mind or
anything else

DATE __/__/__

About my day

Spells, Whats on my mind or anything else

HEY WITCH- MY SKIP DIARY
DATE __/__/__
About my day
Spells, Whats on my mind or anything else

HEY WITCH- MY SKIP DIARY

About my day

Spells, Whats on my mind or anything else

DATE __/__/__

About my day

Spells, Whats on my mind or anything else

DATE __/__/__

About my day

Spells, Whats on my mind or anything else

DATE __/__/__

About my day

Spells, Whats on my mind or anything else

DATE __/__/__

About my day

Spells, Whats on my mind or anything else

DATE __/__/__

About my day

Spells, Whats on my mind or anything else

About my day

Spells, Whats on my mind or anything else

DATE __/__/__

About my day

Spells, Whats on my mind or anything else

DATE __/__/__

About my day

Spells, Whats on my mind or anything else

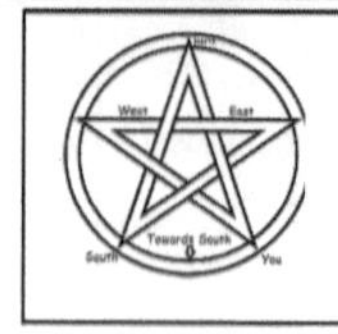

DATE __/__/__

About my day

Spells, Whats on my mind or anything else

DATE __/__/__

About my day

Spells, Whats on my mind or anything else

DATE __/__/__

About my day

Spells, Whats on my mind or anything else

DATE __/__/__

About my day

Spells, Whats on my mind or anything else

DATE __/__/__

About my day

Spells, Whats on my mind or anything else

DATE __/__/__

About my day

Spells, Whats on my mind or anything else

About my day

Spells, Whats on my mind or anything else

DATE __/__/__

About my day

Spells, Whats on my mind or anything else

DATE __/__/__

About my day

**Spells, Whats on my mind or
anything else**

DATE __/__/__

About my day

____

Spells, Whats on my mind or anything else

____

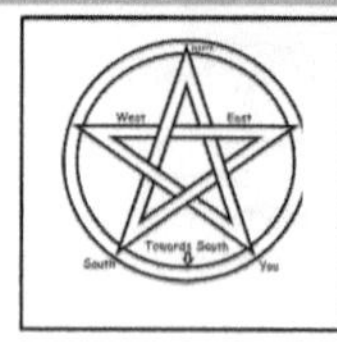

DATE __/__/__

About my day

Spells, Whats on my mind or anything else

About my day

Spells, Whats on my mind or anything else

DATE __/__/__

About my day

Spells, Whats on my mind or anything else

DATE __/__/__

About my day

Spells, Whats on my mind or anything else

About my day

Spells, Whats on my mind or anything else

DATE __/__/__

About my day

Spells, Whats on my mind or anything else

DATE __/__/__

About my day

Spells, Whats on my mind or anything else

DATE __/__/__

About my day

Spells, Whats on my mind or anything else

DATE __/__/__

About my day

Spells, Whats on my mind or anything else

About my day

Spells, Whats on my mind or anything else

HEY WITCH- MY SKIP DIARY

DATE __/__/__

About my day

Spells, Whats on my mind or anything else

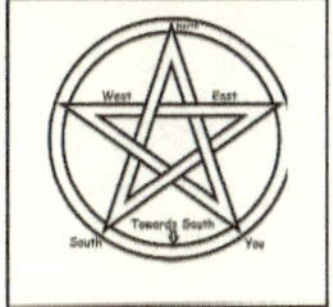

HEY WITCH- MY SKIP DIARY

About my day

Spells, Whats on my mind or anything else

DATE __/__/__

About my day

Spells, Whats on my mind or anything else

DATE __/__/__

About my day

Spells, Whats on my mind or anything else

About my day

Spells, Whats on my mind or anything else

DATE __/__/__

About my day

Spells, Whats on my mind or anything else

DATE __/__/__

About my day

Spells, Whats on my mind or anything else

HEY WITCH- MY SKIP DIARY

DATE __ / __ / __

About my day

Spells, Whats on my mind or anything else

DATE __/__/__

About my day

Spells, Whats on my mind or anything else

DATE __/__/__

About my day

Spells, Whats on my mind or anything else

DATE __/__/__

About my day

Spells, Whats on my mind or anything else

DATE __/__/__

About my day

Spells, Whats on my mind or anything else

HEY WITCH- MY SKIP DIARY

About my day

Spells, Whats on my mind or anything else

DATE __/__/__

About my day

Spells, Whats on my mind or anything else

DATE __/__/__

About my day

Spells, Whats on my mind or anything else

HEY WITCH- MY SKIP DIARY

DATE __ / __ / __

About my day

Spells, Whats on my mind or anything else

About my day

Spells, Whats on my mind or anything else

DATE __/__/__

About my day

Spells, Whats on my mind or anything else

DATE __/__/__

About my day

Spells, Whats on my mind or anything else

DATE __/__/__

About my day

Spells, Whats on my mind or anything else

DATE __/__/__

About my day

Spells, Whats on my mind or anything else

DATE __/__/__

About my day

Spells, Whats on my mind or anything else

DATE __/__/__

About my day

Spells, Whats on my mind or anything else

DATE __/__/__

About my day

Spells, Whats on my mind or anything else

HEY WITCH- MY SKIP DIARY

DATE __/__/__

About my day

Spells, Whats on my mind or anything else

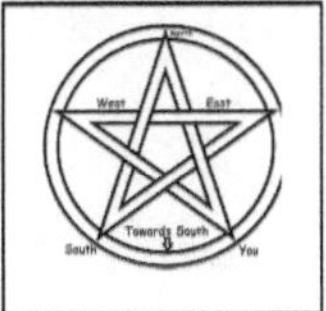

DATE __/__/__

About my day

Spells, Whats on my mind or anything else

DATE __/__/__

About my day

Spells, Whats on my mind or anything else

DATE __/__/__

About my day

Spells, Whats on my mind or anything else

DATE __/__/__

About my day

___

Spells, Whats on my mind or anything else

___

DATE __/__/__

About my day

Spells, Whats on my mind or anything else

DATE __/__/__

About my day

Spells, Whats on my mind or anything else

DATE __ / __ / __

About my day

Spells, Whats on my mind or anything else

DATE __/__/__

About my day

____

**Spells, Whats on my mind or
anything else**

____

DATE __/__/__

About my day

Spells, Whats on my mind or anything else

DATE __/__/__

About my day

Spells, Whats on my mind or
anything else

DATE __ / __ / __

About my day

____

Spells, Whats on my mind or anything else

____

DATE __/__/__

About my day

Spells, Whats on my mind or anything else

DATE __/__/__

About my day

Spells, Whats on my mind or anything else

DATE __/__/__

About my day

Spells, Whats on my mind or anything else

DATE __/__/__

About my day

Spells, Whats on my mind or anything else

DATE _ _ / _ _ / _ _

About my day

Spells, Whats on my mind or anything else

DATE __/__/__

About my day

Spells, Whats on my mind or anything else

DATE __/__/__

About my day

Spells, Whats on my mind or anything else

DATE __/__/__

About my day

Spells, Whats on my mind or anything else

DATE __/__/__

About my day

Spells, Whats on my mind or anything else

DATE __/__/__

About my day

Spells, Whats on my mind or anything else

DATE __/__/__

About my day

Spells, Whats on my mind or anything else

DATE __/__/__

About my day

Spells, Whats on my mind or anything else

DATE __/__/__

About my day

Spells, Whats on my mind or anything else

DATE __/__/__

About my day

Spells, Whats on my mind or anything else

About my day

____

Spells, Whats on my mind or anything else

____

DATE __/__/__

About my day

Spells, Whats on my mind or anything else

DATE __/__/__

About my day

Spells, Whats on my mind or anything else

DATE __ / __ / __

About my day

____

Spells, Whats on my mind or anything else

____

About my day

Spells, Whats on my mind or anything else

DATE __/__/__

About my day

Spells, Whats on my mind or anything else

DATE __/__/__

About my day

Spells, Whats on my mind or anything else

DATE __/__/__

About my day

Spells, Whats on my mind or anything else

DATE __/__/__

About my day

Spells, Whats on my mind or anything else

DATE __/__/__

About my day

Spells, Whats on my mind or anything else

DATE __/__/__

About my day

Spells, Whats on my mind or anything else

DATE __/__/__

About my day

Spells, Whats on my mind or anything else

DATE __/__/__

About my day

Spells, Whats on my mind or anything else

About my day

Spells, Whats on my mind or anything else

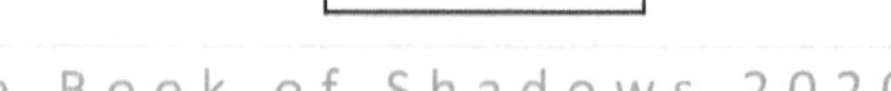

DATE __/__/__

About my day

Spells, Whats on my mind or anything else

DATE __/__/__

About my day

Spells, Whats on my mind or anything else

DATE __/__/__

About my day

Spells, Whats on my mind or anything else

DATE __/__/__

About my day

Spells, Whats on my mind or anything else

DATE __/__/__

About my day

Spells, Whats on my mind or anything else

DATE __/__/__

About my day

Spells, Whats on my mind or anything else

DATE __/__/__

About my day

Spells, Whats on my mind or anything else

DATE __/__/__

About my day

Spells, Whats on my mind or anything else

DATE __/__/__

About my day

Spells, Whats on my mind or anything else

DATE __/__/__

About my day

Spells, Whats on my mind or anything else

DATE __/__/__

About my day

Spells, Whats on my mind or anything else

DATE __/__/__

About my day

Spells, Whats on my mind or anything else

DATE __/__/__

About my day

Spells, Whats on my mind or anything else

DATE __/__/__

About my day

Spells, Whats on my mind or anything else

HEY WITCH- MY SKIP DIARY

DATE __/__/__

About my day

Spells, Whats on my mind or anything else

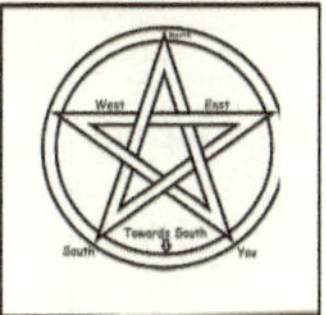

HEY WITCH- MY SKIP DIARY

DATE __/__/__

About my day

Spells, Whats on my mind or anything else

DATE __/__/__

About my day

Spells, Whats on my mind or
anything else

About my day

Spells, Whats on my mind or anything else

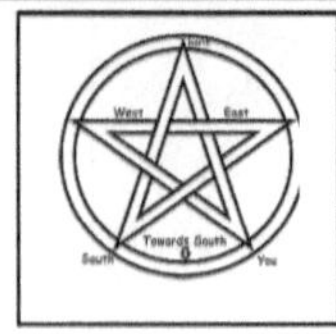

DATE __/__/__

About my day

Spells, Whats on my mind or anything else

DATE __/__/__

About my day

Spells, Whats on my mind or anything else

DATE __/__/__

About my day

Spells, Whats on my mind or anything else

DATE _ _ / _ _ / _ _

About my day

Spells, Whats on my mind or anything else

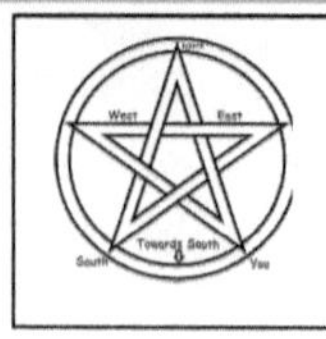

About my day

Spells, Whats on my mind or anything else

DATE __/__/__

About my day

Spells, Whats on my mind or anything else

DATE __/__/__

About my day

Spells, Whats on my mind or anything else

DATE __/__/__

About my day

____

Spells, Whats on my mind or anything else

____

DATE __/__/__

About my day

Spells, Whats on my mind or anything else

DATE __/__/__

About my day

Spells, Whats on my mind or anything else

DATE __/__/__

About my day

Spells, Whats on my mind or anything else

DATE __/__/__

About my day

Spells, Whats on my mind or
anything else

HEY WITCH- MY SKIP DIARY

About my day

Spells, Whats on my mind or anything else

DATE __/__/__

About my day

Spells, Whats on my mind or anything else

DATE __/__/__

About my day

Spells, Whats on my mind or anything else

DATE __/__/__

About my day

____

Spells, Whats on my mind or anything else

____

DATE __/__/__

About my day

Spells, Whats on my mind or anything else

DATE __/__/__

About my day

Spells, Whats on my mind or anything else

DATE __/__/__

About my day

Spells, Whats on my mind or anything else

DATE __/__/__

About my day

Spells, Whats on my mind or anything else

About my day

Spells, Whats on my mind or anything else

DATE __/__/__

About my day

____

Spells, Whats on my mind or anything else

____

HEY WITCH- MY SKIP DIARY

DATE __/__/__

About my day

Spells, Whats on my mind or anything else

DATE __ / __ / __

About my day

Spells, Whats on my mind or anything else

DATE __/__/__

About my day

Spells, Whats on my mind or anything else

DATE __/__/__

About my day

Spells, Whats on my mind or anything else

DATE __/__/__

About my day

Spells, Whats on my mind or anything else

DATE __/__/__

About my day

Spells, Whats on my mind or anything else

DATE __/__/__

About my day

Spells, Whats on my mind or anything else

DATE __/__/__

About my day

Spells, Whats on my mind or anything else

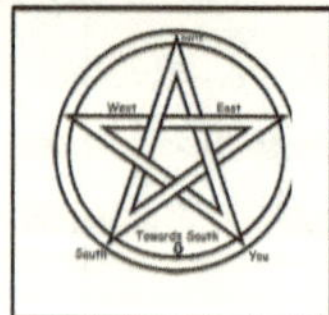

DATE __/__/__

About my day

Spells, Whats on my mind or
anything else

DATE __/__/__

About my day

Spells, Whats on my mind or anything else

About my day

Spells, Whats on my mind or anything else

DATE __/__/__

About my day

Spells, Whats on my mind or anything else

DATE __/__/__

About my day

Spells, Whats on my mind or anything else

DATE __/__/__

About my day

Spells, Whats on my mind or anything else

DATE __/__/__

About my day

Spells, Whats on my mind or anything else

Many thanks for

taking the time to buy, read and write in this book.

The Publisher offsets the carbon footprint of this book by paying for the replanting of trees.

Our planet is important, so please research climate change and do whatever you can to help our planet for example:

Walk or Cycle

Turn off lights etc. when not needed

Don't waste water

Eat less meat, but make sure you still eat enough plant protein foods (fruit, seeds and vegetables)

Campaign your local councils and governments do more to save our planet by stopping fossil fuel use. Campaign for greener energy companies.